MR.BRAVE

MR. BRAVE

by Roger Hargreaves

WORLD INTERNATIONAL
MANCHESTER

Mr Brave is not as strong
as Mr Strong.

He is not as tall as Mr Tall.

But that does not stop him being brave,
as you will soon see.

Now, last Tuesday, Little Miss Bossy invited
Mr Brave to tea.

"AND DON'T BE LATE!" she shouted
down the phone.

It was a very stormy day, but Mr Brave
knew that Little Miss Bossy's temper was worse.

So he set off for Little Miss Bossy's house,
hurrying along as fast as he could
to be sure that he was not late for tea.

Along the way he heard a cry for help.

It was Mr Messy.

He had been blown into the river by the wind.

Mr Brave did not want to be late for Little Miss Bossy
but, being the brave fellow he was,
he jumped in and rescued Mr Messy.

Wet right through,
he hurried along the lane.

Suddenly, he heard someone sobbing loudly.

Who could it be?

It was Little Miss Somersault!

She was balancing on a tightrope
tied between two tall trees!

"Oh, Mr Brave, I'm so lonely," she sobbed.
"Nobody will come and play on my tightrope!
They are all too frightened of heights.
You're so brave, won't you come
and join me?"

Mr Brave looked up at Little Miss Somersault.

Then he thought about Little Miss Bossy,
but, being the brave fellow he was,
he took pity on Little Miss Somersault
and climbed up on to the tightrope.

They chatted away happily for a while
until Mr Brave happened to look down.

"Little Miss Somersault! Look!
The rope is going to snap!
We're going to fall …
and it's such a long way to the bottom.
Oh, calamity! Oh, help!" he cried out in panic.

"Be brave, Mr Brave," said Little Miss Somersault.

And without more ado,
she carried him safely back
down to the ground.

"Oh, thank you," said Mr Brave,
with a sigh of relief.

Little Miss Somersault said goodbye.

And Mr Brave was left on his own,
shaking like a leaf.

"I don't deserve to be called Mr Brave,
I was scared stiff! Thank goodness
nobody knows my secret,"
he said to himself.

And nobody does know his secret,
or do they?

Little Miss Trouble just happened to be
passing and had seen everything.

And what she had seen and heard
had given her an idea.

A very naughty idea!

She grinned a mischievous grin.

"Hey, come here everybody,
come and see this!" she shouted
at the top of her voice.

Very quickly a large crowd gathered.

"I have an announcement,"
announced Little Miss Trouble.
"Did you know that Mr Brave isn't brave at all?"

"No, it can't be true," said the crowd, all together.

"It is true!" said Little Miss Trouble,
"and I'll prove it to you."

"Mr Brave," she continued,
"I dare you to walk across that tightrope!"

Mr Brave looked up at the tightrope.

And all the crowd looked up at the tightrope.

Then all the crowd looked at Mr Brave.

Mr Brave suddenly remembered something.

A very important something.

"Just look at the time!" he cried.
"I'm going to be late
for tea at Little Miss Bossy's!"

"Must dash!" he cried.

And he ran off as quickly as possible.

"Hooray!" cheered the crowd.

And they all clapped and applauded Mr Brave.

Little Miss Trouble looked puzzled.

"Why are you all cheering him?" she cried.
"He ran away! He isn't brave at all!"

"Oh, yes he is!" they all shouted.
"Would you turn up late for tea at
Little Miss Bossy's house?"

Little Miss Trouble thought for a moment.

"Gosh, he is brave after all!" she said in awe.

MR MEN question time – can you help?
10 sets of 4 Mr Men titles to be won!

Thank you for purchasing a Mr Men pocket book. We would be most grateful if you would help us with the answers to a few questions. Each questionnaire received will be placed in a monthly draw – you could win four Mr Men books of your choice and a free bookmark!

Is this the first Mr Men pocket book you have purchased? **Yes** ☐ **No** ☐ (please tick)

If No, how many books do you have in your collection? ___

Have you collected any Little Miss books? **Yes** ☐ **No** ☐ **How many** ___

Where do you usually shop for children's books? **Bookshop** ☐ **Newsagent** ☐ **Supermarket** ☐ **Garden Centre** ☐

Would you be interested in a presentation box to keep your Mr Men books in? **Yes** ☐ **No** ☐

Do you know that there are other types of Mr Men books? **Yes** ☐ **No** ☐

If No, would you be interested in knowing about these? **Yes** ☐ **No** ☐

Apart from Mr Men, who is your favourite children's character? _____

Thank you for your help.

Return this form to: Marketing Department, World International Publishing, Egmont House, PO Box111, 61 Great Ducie Street, Manchester M60 3BL.

Please tick overleaf which four Mr Men books you would like to receive if you are successful in our monthly draw and fill in your name and address details.

Signature of parent or guardian:

We may occasionally wish to advise you of other children's books that we publish. If you would rather we didn't, please tick this box ☐

Tick the 4 Mr Men books you would like to win.

- ☐ 1. Mr Tickle
- ☐ 2. Mr Greedy
- ☐ 3. Mr Happy
- ☐ 4. Mr Nosey
- ☐ 5. Mr Sneeze
- ☐ 6. Mr Bump
- ☐ 7. Mr Snow
- ☐ 8. Mr Messy
- ☐ 9. Mr Topsy-Turvy
- ☐ 10. Mr Silly
- ☐ 11. Mr Uppity
- ☐ 12. Mr Small
- ☐ 13. Mr Daydream
- ☐ 14. Mr Forgetful
- ☐ 15. Mr Jelly

- ☐ 16. Mr Noisy
- ☐ 17. Mr Lazy
- ☐ 18. Mr Funny
- ☐ 19. Mr Mean
- ☐ 20. Mr Chatterbox
- ☐ 21. Mr Fussy
- ☐ 22. Mr Bounce
- ☐ 23. Mr Muddle
- ☐ 24. Mr Dizzy
- ☐ 25. Mr Impossible
- ☐ 26. Mr Strong
- ☐ 27. Mr Grumpy
- ☐ 28. Mr Clumsy
- ☐ 29. Mr Quiet
- ☐ 30. Mr Rush

- ☐ 31. Mr Tall
- ☐ 32. Mr Worry
- ☐ 33. Mr Nonsense
- ☐ 34. Mr Wrong
- ☐ 35. Mr Skinny
- ☐ 36. Mr Mischief
- ☐ 37. Mr Clever
- ☐ 38. Mr Busy
- ☐ 39. Mr Slow
- ☐ 40. Mr Brave
- ☐ 41. Mr Grumble
- ☐ 42. Mr Perfect
- ☐ 43. Mr Cheerful

Your name _____

Address _____

_____

_____ Postcode _____